WHAT MESS?

TOP GOES THIS WAY

RIGHT HAND

LEFT HAND

BROOM BASICS

BOTTOM GOES THIS WAY

DIRT GOES UNDER BED

CLEAN SOCKS GO ON FEET

DIRTY SOCKS GO IN LAUNDRY

How to FOLD a SHIRT

1

2

the CLOTHES HANGER WAS invented in 1903 BY ALBERT J. PARKHOUSE, WHO WOULD PROBABLY NOT MIND AT ALL if YOU USED ONE ONCE IN A WHILE

LINE UP STUFFED ANIMALS ON YOUR BED SO THEY CAN TALK OR NAP

PURRRRR

CLUTEROLOGY

VOLCANOES

FUN WITH FUNGI

Turn JUNK into Art

Basics of Purification

CHAOS THEORY

Family Dynamics of Bugs

GOOD GNUS

USE AN IMMOVABLE OBJECT to keep Books in Place

MOST TOYS NEED HELP GETTING IN

Look at this room,
it's in such distress,
you'd have to clean up
just to call it a mess.
The clutter and filth
put our house in disgrace.
What's the matter with you?
Can't you clean up this place?

Your stuff and your things
are in such disarray,
we just can't believe
you live here this way.
Your shoes in a pile,
your shirts in a bunch,
and there in that corner,
is that yesterday's lunch?

You take off your pants
and you just let them fall,
you throw dirty shirts
and they stick to the wall.
Your stinky old running shoes
got up and ran,
outstunk by your underwear
hung from the fan.

You used to think monsters hid under your bed,
now we think so too, but it smells like they're dead.
And even though this one looks strong as an ox,
his fatal mistake was eating your socks.

The clothing we bought
at those fancy new stores
now lies in a heap
growing fungus and spores.
While the custom-made closet
we built for these garments
has become a state refuge
for vermin and varmints.

There's lizards and lemurs
and hideous hedgehogs,
wombats and weasels
and Brazilian tree frogs.
I'm putting my foot down,
this place is a zoo.
What's this I stepped in?
It feels like gnu poo.

For your birthday we gave you

those fancy new blocks,

but you've cast them aside

and just use the box.

It houses some creature,

it's hard to tell what,

we don't want to know,

so please keep it shut.

We'd like you to tell us, your mom and your dad,
how it got in this state, how your room got this bad.
We brought you the mop, the vacuum and broom.
Now why, my dear child, won't you clean up this room?

Mom, Dad,
you don't understand.
It's not random filth,
everything's planned!
The muck and the mess
and the clothes that are cruddy,
they all play a part
in my homework and study.

I've got math, I've got science,
I've got all of those classes,
not to mention a study
of stinky shoe gases.
The crud and the critters,
they all play a part,
and if it's not science,
I just call it art.

Those clothes aren't heaped up just because I'm a pig,
I'm actually creating an archaeological dig.
In a couple of years I'll give you a chance
to dig and discover my petrified pants.

3RD GRADE

2ND GRADE

1ST GRADE

KINDERGARTEN

That isn't just vermin down under the rugs,
I'm studying a family of misbehaved bugs.
On my knees all day Tuesday I got a bad blister
while watching a cockroach torment his young sister.

And my underwear flung on the fan is, of course,
just a method to study centrifugal force.
As they spin round and round I can measure the flows
of the air by the smells that I smell with my nose.

I'm not the first person with a closet of fur,
but mine are alive, that's what they prefer.
And while all their doo-doo is nasty to noses,
just wait 'til you see how it growses the roses.

That food in the corner,
all covered with green,
will save you big money,
come next Halloween.

With time it will turn
into sticky brown snacks
perfect for filling
those trick-or-treat sacks.

And finally here's something
of which I'm most proud
but cover your ears,
the noise could be loud.
It'll clear out your noses,
if not the whole room,
when I pour in the vinegar
and watch it go...

Although that experiment was really a blast,
it cleaned out my room just a little too fast,
Now all my pet projects have turned to debris
and taught me a lesson from up in a tree.

I'm done with excuses, it's time to confess,
that room was a pigsty, a big moldy mess.
As soon as I locate the mop and the broom,
I'll make an experiment of cleaning my room!

Thanks to Adam Lichtenheld, whose poem "The Room of Doom" inspired this book.

TO JAN, FOR HER WISDOM, IMAGINATION, AND LOVE

Little, Brown and Company

Hachette Book Group
237 Park Avenue, New York, NY 10017
Visit our website at www.lb-kids.com

Little, Brown and Company is a division of Hachette Book Group, Inc.
The Little, Brown name and logo are trademarks of Hachette Book Group, Inc.

The publisher is not responsible for websites (or their content) that are not owned by the publisher.

First Edition: October 2012
First published in hardcover as *What's With This Room?* in September 2005 by Little, Brown and Company

Library of Congress Cataloging-in-Publication Data

Lichtenheld, Tom.
  [What's with this room?]
  What mess? / by Tom Lichtenheld.—1st [pbk.] ed.
    p. cm.
  Summary: A discussion between a boy and his parents about a bedroom that is so dirty he would "have to clean up just to call it a mess" ends with a blast.
  ISBN 978-0-316-20123-0 (pbk.)
  [1. Stories in rhyme. 2. Cleanliness—Fiction. 3. Parent and child—Fiction. 4. Humorous stories.] I. Title.
  PZ8.3.L596Wg 2012
  [E]—dc23
                                    2012009407

10 9 8 7 6 5 4 3 2 1

SC

Printed in China

The illustrations for this book were done in ink, watercolor, colored pencil, pastels, and toe jam.
The text was set in Fritz, and the display type is hand lettered.
No gnus were harmed in the making of this book.

Book design by Tom Lichtenheld

OTHER BOOKS BY TOM LICHTENHELD

WHAT ARE YOU SO GRUMPY ABOUT?
Named one of the best children's books of the year by *Child* magazine
A *Kirkus Reviews* ★ Starred Review

SHARK VS. TRAIN
by Chris Barton, illustrated by Tom Lichtenheld
A *New York Times* Bestseller
A *Kirkus Reviews* ★ Starred Review
A *Publishers Weekly* ★ Starred Review
A *School Library Journal* ★ Starred Review

TOM LICHTENHELD folds his underwear neatly and keeps his colored pencils lined up so they make a perfect rainbow. He enjoys vacuuming, but it scares the cat, so he only does it once a year. Other than that, he's kind of a slob. Tom lives in Illinois with his wife, Jan, and their cat, Scooter. Jan comes up with some of the best ideas in Tom's books. Scooter comes up with hairballs. (Scooter doesn't realize that hairballs lead to vacuuming.) Tom's website is www.tomlichtenheld.com.